CUDDLE ME HAPPY
A Collection of Stories for Sharing

LITTLE TIGER PRESS
An imprint of Magi Publications
1 The Coda Centre, 189 Munster Road,
London SW6 6AW
www.littletigerpress.com

First published in Great Britain 2010
This volume copyright
© Magi Publications 2010
Cover illustration copyright
© Caroline Pedler 2007

All rights reserved
Printed in China
ISBN 978-1-84895-001-6

LTP/1800/0247/0611

2 4 6 8 10 9 7 5 3

DORA'S EGGS
Julie Sykes
Illustrated by Jane Chapman
First published in Great Britain 1997
by Little Tiger Press,
an imprint of Magi Publications
Text copyright © Julie Sykes 1997
Illustrations copyright © Jane Chapman 1997

HAPPY BIRTHDAY, DOTTY!
Tim Warnes
First published in Great Britain 2003
by Little Tiger Press,
an imprint of Magi Publications
Text and illustrations copyright
© Tim Warnes 2003

HUNGRY HARRY
Joanne Partis
First published in Great Britain 2000
by Little Tiger Press,
an imprint of Magi Publications
Text and illustrations copyright
© Joanne Partis 2000

BIG BEARS CAN!
David Bedford
Illustrated by Gaby Hansen
First published in Great Britain 2001
by Little Tiger Press,
an imprint of Magi Publications
Text copyright © David Bedford 2001
Illustrations copyright © Gaby Hansen 2001

Cuddle me Happy

A Collection of Stories for Sharing

LITTLE TIGER PRESS
London

Contents

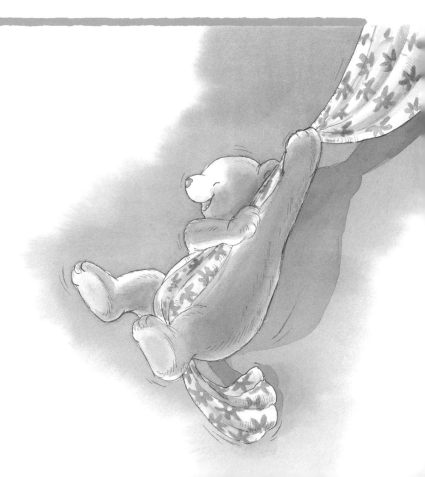

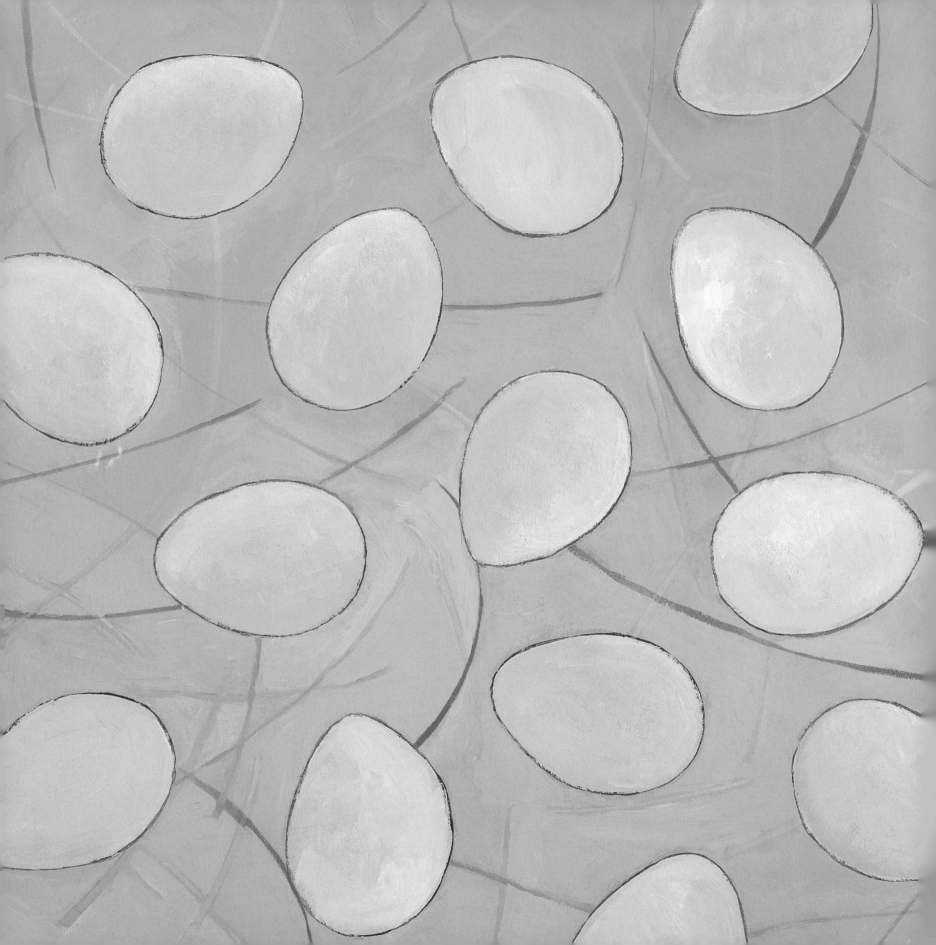

DORA'S EGGS

by Julie Sykes

illustrated by Jane Chapman

Dora was sitting on a nest of eggs.
They were shiny brown and smooth
to touch.
"These are my very first eggs,"
clucked Dora proudly.
"I must get all my friends to
come and admire them."

Dora climbed out of the hen house
and into the farmyard.
"Who shall I visit first?" she asked.
"I know! I'll go and find Doffy Duck."

Dora hopped over the fence and across
the field until she reached the pond.
"Hello, Doffy," called Dora. "Would you
like to come and see my eggs?"
"I can't come now," quacked Doffy.
"I'm teaching my babies to swim."

Dora stood watching the ducklings
splashing around and learning to paddle.
Somehow she felt a bit less excited.
"My eggs are nice," she thought.
"But those fluffy ducklings are
much nicer."

Dora felt just a little sad as she trotted
off to the sty to visit Penny Pig.
"Hello, Penny," she clucked. "Would you
like to come and see my eggs?"
But Penny didn't hear. She was having
too much fun, tumbling around with her
wriggly piglets.

Dora gave a little sigh.
"My eggs are nice," she said. "But
those wriggly piglets are much nicer."

Dora gave another little sigh as she climbed the hill to find Sally Sheep. "Would you like to come and see my eggs?" she asked Sally. "Not today," bleated Sally. "I'm too busy keeping an eye on my lambs."

Dora looked at the lambs, frolicking in the field. She felt rather glum. "My eggs are nice," she thought. "But those playful lambs are much nicer."

Very sadly, Dora walked back to the farmyard.
On her way she bumped into Daisy Dog.
"Hello, Daisy," clucked Dora. "Would you like
to come and see my eggs?"
"Sorry, Dora," barked Daisy, wagging her tail.
"I can't come now. I'm taking my puppies
for a walk."

Dora was beginning to feel
quite miserable.
"My eggs are nice," she said.
"But those puppies out
for a walk are much nicer."

In the farmyard Dora stopped
at the cowshed. She wished she
felt happier, but perhaps Clarissa
the Cow would cheer her up.
"Would you like to see my eggs?"
she called.

"Sssh," mooed Clarissa softly, nodding her head at the straw. Snuggled up by her feet and fast asleep was a newborn calf. Dora felt like crying. "My eggs are nice," she whispered. "But that little calf, all snuggled up, is much nicer."

21

Dora walked back across the yard in the
sunlight and climbed into the hen house.
Her eggs were just as she left them,
smooth and brown and very still.
"My eggs are nice," sighed Dora, fluffing
out her feathers. "But everyone else's
babies are *much* nicer."

Very sadly, Dora settled
herself down on to
her nest . . .

CRACK!

Dora jumped up in surprise.

"Oh no!" cried Dora. "I've broken them!"
Tears began to roll down her face.
They splashed on to the nest and over
the cracked eggs. As each tear fell,
the cracks grew wider and wider until
suddenly . . .

. . . up popped a fluffy head,
then another, and another.

Soon the nest was full of
tiny chicks.
"Cheep, cheep," the chicks
squeaked. "Cheep, cheep."
Dora stopped crying and
stared.

It didn't matter that the eggs were broken.
The new chicks were everything Dora had
ever wanted!
Proudly she strutted out into the farmyard,
and one by one the chicks followed after her.
All the animals stopped and stared.

"Why, Dora!" quacked Doffy.
"They're as fluffy as my ducklings!"
"And wriggly like my piglets,"
 oinked Penny.
"They're as playful as my lambs,"
 baaed Sally.
"And you can take them for walks –
 just like my puppies," barked Daisy.
"But best of all," mooed Clarissa,
"your chicks can snuggle up to you,
 like my calf snuggles up to me."
"Cluck," said Dora happily, agreeing
 with her friends. "My eggs were
 nice, but my chicks are much,
 much nicer!"

32

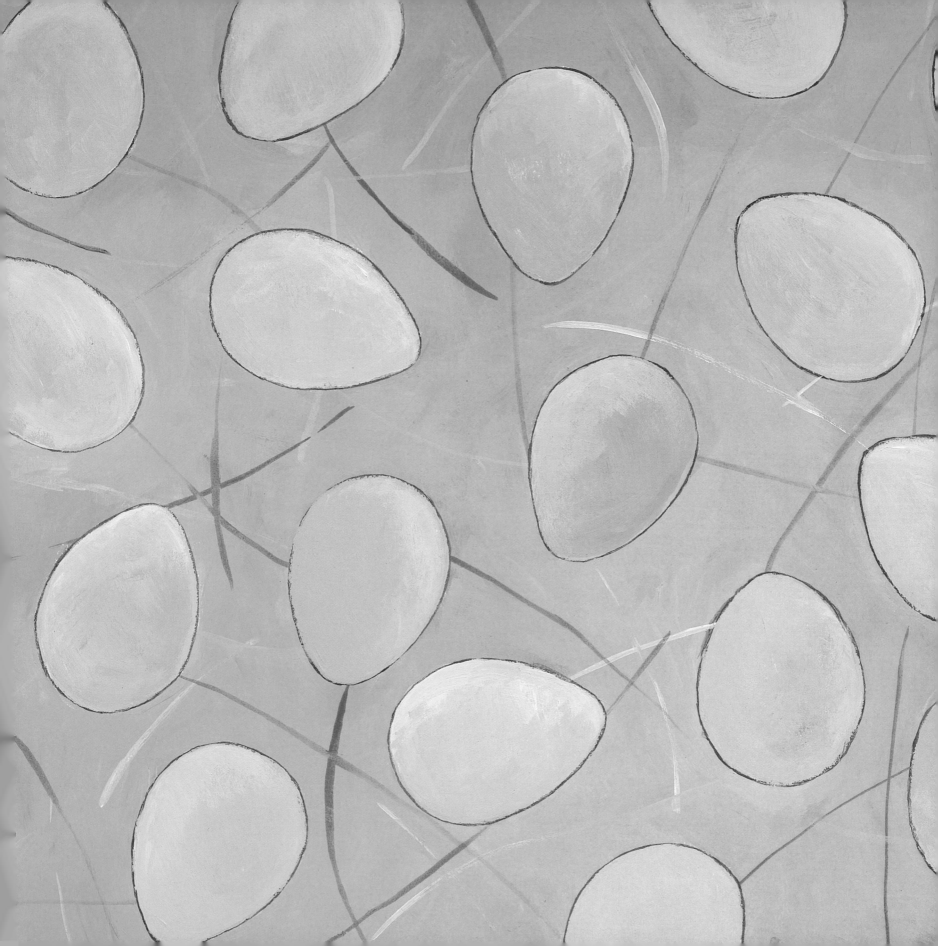

Tim Warnes

Happy Birthday, Dotty!

Dotty was very excited.

It was her birthday.

She had lots of cards
to open. But where were
all Dotty's friends?

41

Dotty went to find Pip the mouse.
Instead she found a little round
present with her name on it!

What could it be?

Happy Birthday
Dotty!
Love from
Pip the mouse x

Hooray!

A bouncy ball!

As she chased after it,
Dotty spotted an arrow
on the floor. It pointed
to another and another.

It was a birthday trail!
Dotty followed the arrows . . .

. . . to the sandpit, where there was *another* parcel. Dotty read the label. "Happy Birthday, Dotty, love from Tommy the tortoise."

What was it?

Delicious!

A yummy bone!

Dotty hurried across
the garden, following
the arrows to . . .

. . . Susie's apple tree.
Leaning against
her nest was
another present!

Yippee!

It was a kite from Susie!

But Susie wasn't there to help fly it.

Where was everyone?

Dotty was puzzled.
Taking all her presents,
she skipped along the trail
of arrows to . . .

. . .Whiskers the rabbit's hutch.
Dotty saw another funny-shaped present.
She read, "Happy Birthday, Dotty,
love from Whiskers."

Dotty began to
unwrap it . . .

Wow!
A trike!

Dotty squealed with delight. She popped all her presents into the trailer. She'd had lots of surprises, but still Dotty's friends were nowhere to be seen.

Where could they be? Maybe they had followed the arrows too. Dotty climbed on to her shiny new trike and . . .

WHEEE!
She went to look for her friends.

Suddenly the trail ended.

Dotty was amazed to find . . .

. . . the
BIGGEST PRESENT
she had ever seen!

Dotty danced round
and round in circles.
What could this be?

"Surprise!
Happy Birthday, Dotty!"

Harry Frog was feeling hungry.
"What's for dinner?" he asked his mum.
"Well, I think you're old enough to look for
your own food now," said Mummy Frog.

"Brilliant!" cried Harry, and off
he leaped across the lily pond . . .

. . . till he came to some tall reeds. "There's sure to be something tasty here," said Harry, licking his lips.

Sure enough, there was a delicious-looking dragonfly. Harry was just about to jump when . . .

. . . the dragonfly flew off, high into the air.
"You can't eat me!" she called.
"I'm much too quick for you."

Harry was wondering
what to do next when
suddenly he saw . . .

. . . a big juicy caterpillar
on a twig above him.

"Goody, goody, dinner at last!" cried Harry, but when he flicked out his long tongue to catch it . . .

. . . the caterpillar laughed. "You can't eat me!" she said. "My hairs would tickle your tongue."

74

"Never mind, I'll find something soon," said Harry.
He bounced on until he met . . .

. . . a scrumptious-looking snail crawling towards him.

"Yummy, yummy," said Harry, but when he reached it . . .

. . . the snail's head suddenly disappeared!
"You can't eat me!" said the
snail from inside its shell.
"I'm much too clever."

Harry was getting hungrier and hungrier.
He was just about to give up and go
home to his mum, when he spotted . . .

. . . a squirmy worm,
wriggling along.
"Now's my chance!" cried
Harry, but just as he was
about to catch the worm
in his big wide mouth . . .

. . . it slithered down into
a wormhole.
"You can't eat me!"
shouted the worm. "I'm
too squiggly and squirmy."

Harry felt very fed up. He would go home to his mum. But just as he turned to hop back, he saw something he'd never seen before . . .

It didn't look too quick . . .

It didn't look too tickly . . .

It didn't look too clever . . .

And it didn't look
too squiggly and
squirmy.

In fact it looked . . .

. . . absolutely delicious!

And, what was more . . .

...there was

enough for everyone!

David Bedford *and* Gaby Hansen

Big Bears Can!

Big Bear had to look after
Little Bear when Mummy
Bear went out.
"Do I have to?" asked Big Bear.
"Yes," said Mummy Bear.
"Just keep the house tidy.
I won't be long."

"What can Big Bears do?" asked Little Bear
when Mummy Bear had gone.
"Big Bears can do *everything*," said Big Bear.
"Can they stand on their heads?"
"Yes they can," said Big Bear.

"See!"

"But they can't do *this*," said Little Bear . . .

BOING! BOING!

"Of course they can,"
said Big Bear. "That's easy."

BOING!

"Oops!"

"Can you fix the springs?"
asked Little Bear.
"Yes," said Big Bear.
"I can."

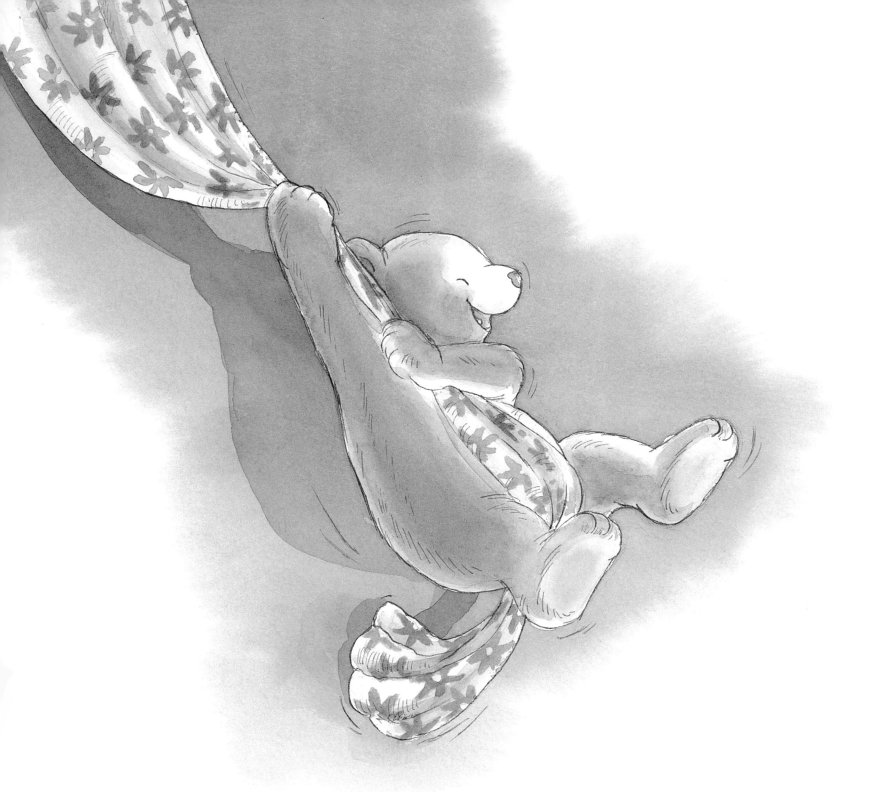

"But you can't do *this*," said Little Bear. "No way."

"Big Bears don't swing," said
Big Bear. "That would be silly."
"You're too big to swing,
anyway," said Little
Bear.

"NO I'M NOT," roared Big Bear. "Watch this!"

"Look out!"
said Little Bear.
"You're too heavy!"

"You've squashed Mummy's flowers, too," said Little Bear. "Can you fix everything?"
"I *hope* I can," said Big Bear.

"But you can't make
tunnels like this,"
said Little Bear.

"I don't want to make tunnels," said Big Bear. "I'm going to sit quietly until Mummy comes back."

"Big Bears *can't* do everything," sang Little Bear. "Big Bears *can't*, Big Bears *can't*, Big Bears CAN'T do everything." "YES THEY CAN!" said Big Bear.

"This is fun, isn't it!" said Big Bear.
"HERE COMES MUMMY," shouted
Little Bear. "She's going to be very angry."

"Big Bears can't hide," said Little Bear.

"Yes they can," said Big Bear. "Move over so I can squeeze in beside you."

"There's not enough room," said Little Bear. "Mummy will see you."

112

"Look at Mummy's face," said Little Bear. "She's very, very, VERY angry." "Big Bears can't get told off," whispered Big Bear. "Can they?"

YES THEY CAN!

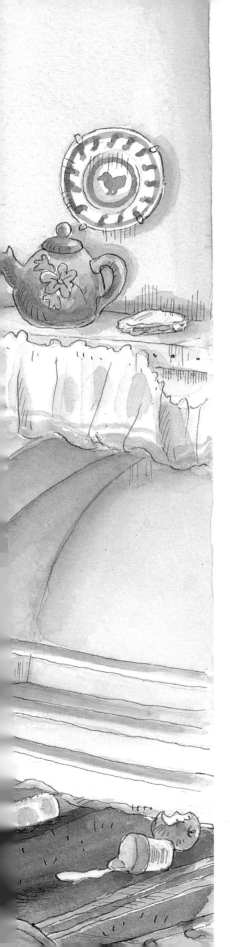

Poor Big Bear. If only Little Bear
could make him feel better.
"Can Big Bears have hugs?" asked
Little Bear.

"Yes," said Big Bear.

"Big Bears can!"